# MEET THE PLANETS

Caryl Hart

Illustrated by **Bethan Woollvin**

BLOOMSBURY
CHILDREN'S BOOKS

LONDON  OXFORD  NEW YORK  NEW DELHI  SYDNEY

The sun shines so bright in the daytime
but when the moon comes out at night,
we see loads of beautiful twinkling stars
as we switch off the warm bedroom light.

It's ever so hard to imagine,
since stars really look kind of small,
that each one's a planet, a sun or a moon –
they're not shining sequins at all!

So . . .

Let's go on a fabulous journey
and meet **all** the **planets** up high.
It's too far to go in a car or a bus . . .

so we'll climb into a rocket and fly!

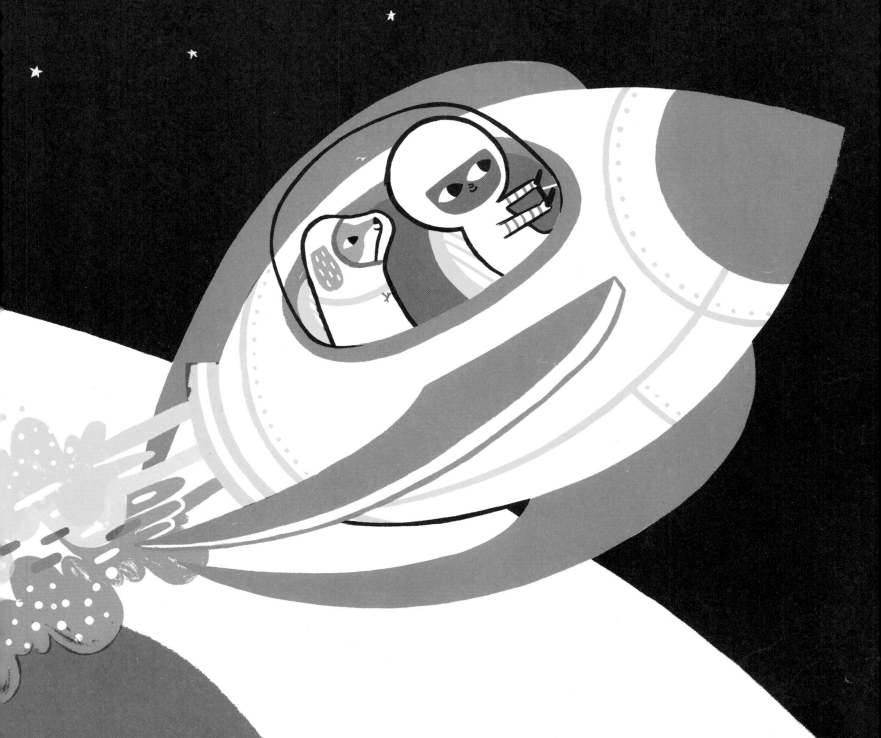

Hello, I'm **THE SUN** – nice to meet you!
I'm the **biggest** thing up in the sky.
I'm friendly but don't get **too close** now
or I'll **frizzle** you up to a fry!

My heat keeps you **warm** in the daytime.
My light helps plants grow wild and green.
But, be careful, I'm really a
**great ball of fire** –
the HOTTEST and FIERCEST
you've seen!

I'm **MERCURY** –
bet you can't CATCH me!
I zip round the sun at top speed.
At fifty kilometres per second –
I'm a very FAST planet indeed.

Wheeeeeeeeeeeeeeee!

Hello there, my lovelies, I'm **VENUS** –
like the **goddess** of beauty you see.
But looks can be somewhat **deceiving** –
I'm as **deadly** and FIERCE as can be.

I'm covered in spitting **volcanoes.**
I'm blistering **hot** night and day.
So, although I'm your nice next-door **neighbour,**
it's best you **don't** come round to play!

Hello, I'm the **EARTH** – you must know me.
I'm coloured a lovely **green-blue**.
On my surface live **millions** of people
and **one** of those people is . . .

## YOU!

I have **oceans** and **forests** and **mountains**,
clean **air** and fresh **water** to drink.
There are no other planets quite like me
so you're **LUCKY** to have me, I think.

Shh! I'm the silver **MOON**, darling –
I keep **watch** while you're tucked up in bed.
But look upwards and sometimes you'll see me –
a ghost in broad **daylight** instead!

Howdy, I'm **MARS** – howya doin?
Most folk around here call me RED.
It's because of this rust-coloured dust
that these pesky winds blow round my head.

It's super cold here in the winter.
There's NO water or food – nope, just ice.
But climb my volcano, it's real super high,
and the view from up there is real nice.

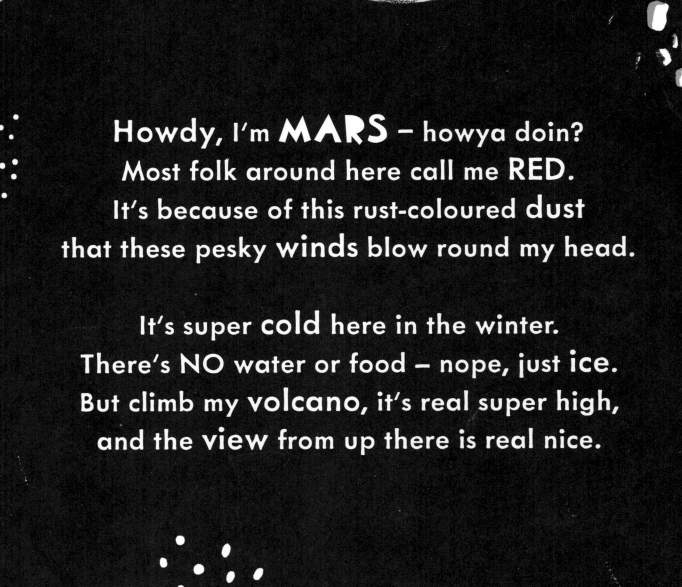

I'm **JUPITER** – king of the planets.
I'm one **giant gaseous ball**.
But don't try to land with your spaceship,
for there's no **solid** ground here at all.

Ho, ho! I'm the **biggest** of planets.
My moon **GANYMEDE** is big too.
We've had this large **girth** since the time of our birth,

My name's **SATURN** –
oh, don't you just love me?
You have to **agree**, I look nice.
Just look at my **RINGS**, aren't they sparkly?
They shimmer with crushed rock and ice!

You humans can't help but **admire** me.
I'm the **prettiest** planet you've seen.
So be sure to take hundreds of pictures
and bow down to your **beautiful** queen!

I'm **URANUS** – golly, I'm f-freezing!
I'm a great swirling windy ice ball.
It's a shame you can't land and **explore** me
but there's **NO rock** in my middle at all!

The name's **NEPTUNE** – *Ice Giant* they call me.
My freezing **skies** make me look **blue**.
It gets **lonely** out here, all this **way** from the earth,
so I'm mightily **pleased** to see YOU!

Yoo hoo! It's me! Little **PLUTO** –
I'm a tiny dwarf planet you know.
And, look, this is **CHARON** my buddy,
she's with me wherever I go!

And now it is time to head **homewards** –
back to **EARTH** where our long **journey** ends.
We've had such an **awesome** adventure
and made lots of wonderful **friends**.

So next time that you snuggle down quietly,
look out at the twinkling night sky.
You'll see ALL your friends smiling downwards –
why not give them a wave and shout, "Hi!"?